Enfield Libraries

ENFIELD CENTRAL LIBRARY
CECIL ROAD
ENFIELD EN2 6TW
Lending: 020 8379 8366
Reference: 020 8379 8391
Music: 020 8379 8392

- 5 JAN 2006

Please remember that this item will attract overdue charges if not returned by the latest date stamped above. You may renew it in person, by telephone or by post quoting the bar code number and your library card number.

www.enfield.gov.uk

780.6 BAC

The New Novello Choral Edition

JOHANN SEBASTIAN BACH
Easter Oratorio
Oster Oratorium
BWV 249

for soprano, alto, tenor and bass soloists, SATB choir and orchestra

Vocal score

Edited with a new English translation by
Neil Jenkins

Order No: NOV 090849

NOVELLO PUBLISHING LIMITED
8/9 Frith Street, London W1D 3JB

Cover illustration: the first page of the autograph score of the *Easter Oratorio*. Reproduced by permission of Staatsbibliothek zu Berlin - Preußischer Kulturbesitz - Musikabteilung mit Mendelssohn-Archive (Berlin State Library - Prussian Cultural Asset - Music Department with Mendelssohn Archive) [Mus. ms. Bach P34, Bl 2r]

© 2003 Novello & Company Limited

Published in Great Britain by Novello Publishing Limited
Head office: 8/9 Frith Street, LONDON, W1D 3JB
Tel +44 (0)20 7434 0066   Fax +44 (0)20 7287 6329

Sales and Hire: Music Sales Distribution Centre
Newmarket Road, Bury St Edmunds, Suffolk, IP33 3YB
Tel +44 (0)1284 702600   Fax +44 (0)1284 768301

www.chesternovello.com   e-mail: music@musicsales.co.uk

All rights reserved   Printed in Great Britain

No part of this publication may be copied or reproduced in any form or by any means without the prior permission of Novello & Company Limited.

It is requested that on all concert notices and programmes acknowledgement is made to 'The New Novello Choral Edition'. Orchestral material is available on hire from the Publisher. Permission to reproduce the Preface of this Edition must be obtained from the Publisher.

CONTENTS

Preface			i
1	Sinfonia		1
2	Duet & Chorus	Come swiftly and hasten *Kommt, eilet und laufet*	9
3	Recitative	How cold the human heart! *O kalter Männer Sinn!*	26
4	Soprano Aria	Welcome are the precious spices *Seele, deine Spezereien*	28
5	Recitative	Here is the tomb *Hier ist die Gruft*	36
6	Tenor Aria	Softly shall my eyes be closing *Sanfte soll mein Todeskummer*	37
7	Recitative	Ah! How I long and pray for that appointed day *Indessen seufzen wir mit brennender Begier*	44
8	Alto Aria	Tell me now in haste *Saget mir geschwinde*	46
9	Recitative	Let us rejoice *Wir sind erfreut*	52
10	Chorus	Praise and thanks let us sing to Christ the King *Preis und Dank bleibe, Herr, dein Lobgesang*	53

APPENDIX

11	Chorale	The strife is o'er, the battle won *Es hat mit uns nun keine Not*	63

PREFACE

HISTORY AND ORIGINS OF THE WORK

During his time in Leipzig, Bach composed much celebratory music, including birthday odes for members of the ruling family. As these were destined to receive single performances, it is not surprising to find movements from them reappearing in the many church cantatas which he had to provide for the Thomaskirche. Thus a large work like the *Christmas Oratorio* is principally made up out of at least three celebratory birthday cantatas.[1]

The *Easter Oratorio* started life as a secular birthday cantata for Christian, Duke of Sachs-Weißenfels with the opening text *Entfliehet, verschwindet, entweichet, ihr Sorgen* [BWV 249a] and was performed on 23rd February 1725. As with all of these birthday odes, it opened and closed with loud celebratory choruses employing the town's trumpeters and drums; such pieces were sometimes performed in the open air, where the instrumentation was particularly effective. Within six weeks the music reappeared with a new, sacred text as the cantata on Easter Sunday, 1 April 1725, even retaining the instrumentation of the original. The speed at which the transformation took place suggests not only that this was always Bach's intention, but also that a text (possibly by Picander) for the sacred version had already been prepared.[2]

Bach reused the music for a second secular purpose on 25th August 1726, with a text by Picander, *Verjaget, zerstreuet, zerrüttet ihr Sterne* (BWV 249b), as a celebratory birthday cantata for Count Joachim Friedrich von Flemming.[3] This version is now lost.

In the mid-1730s, during Bach's tenure as Cantor in Leipzig, he revised the sacred version again and gave it the title *Oratorium* by which it is now best known. Some changes are very minor: reallocation of the instrumental obbligati (reflecting the forces available at the time) and reworkings of the text and the vocal underlay (particularly the choral bass line to the final chorus); others are more significant, such as the addition of five bars (bb.68-72) at the end of No.8. Changes continued through the late 1730s or 1740s when chorus parts were added to No.2 (originally a tenor and bass duet).

It seems that, at this time, Bach was intent on providing a library of music for the church's major festivals to meet his future needs, so that he could be free to move on to other creative forms, such as *Die Kunst der Fuge* and the *Clavier-übung III*. It is significant that the three works bearing the title *Oratorium* – the *Christmas Oratorio* (BWV 248) and *Ascension Oratorio* (BWV 11) as well as this reworking – all date from the same period of concentrated activity in 1734/5.

Unlike the *Passions* and the *Christmas Oratorio*, the *Easter Oratorio* does not use Gospel text. The recitatives, which are where you would expect to find the Easter story unfolded in biblical narrative, are also the work of the librettist. At one stage in an early manuscript, the four soloists were identified with the characters in the Gospel narrative, with Peter and John being the tenor and bass, and the two Marys the soprano and alto. But these were dropped in the final manuscript. It seems that there was no time in the Leipzig Easter Day service for a cantata longer than the normal weekly one. Philipp Spitta, in an effort to account for the lack of Gospel text given to the Evangelist, discovered that, in the morning service at Leipzig on Easter Day

> …there was only time for a piece of music on the scale of a cantata, which was not allowed to be in two parts either, as the Sanctus still had to be performed after the sermon. As Bach could not compose the Gospel account to the extent that would have seemed desirable to him and to which it had been dealt with by Vopelius (in his *Neu Leipziger Gesangbuch*), he might have preferred the form of an Italian oratorio, which carries different expectations from the start, to taking a fragment out of the Gospel account.[4]

So this work, whilst being a reflection of the Easter events in the Garden at the empty tomb, has no time to expand on them in the same way that, say, Heinrich Schütz had in his *The Resurrection Story* (*Auferstehungs-Historia*) in the previous century. It remains in essence therefore, despite its title, a cantata rather than an oratorio.

EDITORIAL PROCEDURE

TEXT

The German text is newly translated. There are places in the arias (particularly bb. 30-31, 48-49 of no. 4 and elsewhere) where I have found that Bach's original underlay, used in the secular version, suits the English version best.

MUSIC

The musical text of this *performing* edition is derived from the manuscript, the *Neuen Bach-Ausgabe* and the *Stuttgarter Bach-Ausgabe* and represents Bach's final version. I have also consulted the *Neuen Bach-Ausgabe* for a comparison with the musical text of the original versions of the arias and choruses in BWV 249a, and to compare the changes Bach made to the vocal text and its underlay. The vocal bass-line in No. 10 observes all the changes made in the 1730s. Likewise the adagio section of No. 1 includes all the appoggiaturas inserted at a later stage into the string parts.

The first vocal movement underwent a number of revisions by Bach, and there are three ways of performing this movement:

A   *Tenor and Bass duet* - Soloists sing to bar 160 and then D.S. to a Fine at bar 120 (the earliest version from 1725);

B   *Soloists and Chorus* - Tenor and Bass soloists sing to bar 160 (chorus *tacet*). Performers ignore *Dal Segno* instruction. Chorus sing from bar 184 to end of movement. This solution, a compromise between Bach's earliest and last-known reworking, was proposed by Wilhelm Rust[5]. Whether Bach ever performed it like this is not known. The editor's preference is for this hybrid version, because it introduces us first to the two protagonists, Peter and John, running to the tomb; and then introduces the Chorus of Believers at the da capo;

C   *Soloists and Chorus* - By the time of Bach's last performances the soloists only sang in the middle section (bb.120-160), flanked by the chorus singing at the opening and conclusion of the movement (bb.24-96, 184-256). This version possibly represents Bach's final solution for this movement.

In this edition the layout of this movement allows for any of these three possible versions.

Unlike Bach's other Eastertide cantatas, BWV 6, 31, 66, 145 and 158, the *Easter Oratorio* has no concluding chorale. Although this is not exceptional among Bach's cantatas, it is not known whether a suitable standard well-known chorale would have been inserted at this point (and therefore not shown in Bach's manuscript). For occasions when it is deemed appropriate to end the work in a way that is proportionate to the overall structure, as opposed to the more abrupt ending shown in the manuscript, a chorale is provided in an Appendix to this edition.

I have followed the suggestion of Diethard Hellman[6] by using the closing chorale from Cantata 130 *Herr Gott, dich loben alle wir* transposed up a tone, and with a German text from the Easter hymn *Weil unser Trost, der Herre Christ, an diesem Tag erstanden ist* by Peter von Hagen. The instrumentation of this chorale is the same as that of the *Easter Oratorio*. For an English translation I have used two verses of the well-known Easter Hymn *The strife is o'er, the battle won* (17th century, tr. Francis Pott). The chorale melody is a compound time version of the Old Hundredth (better known as *All people that on earth do dwell*).

EDITORIAL MARKINGS

All editorial markings are shown in brackets with the exception of editorial slurs which have a line through them (cut-slurs).

Dynamics Bach used dynamics sparingly in the *Easter Oratorio*. Although they can mean what we expect them to mean - as in No. 2 bars 2-4, and 252-254 where they indicate a sudden change of dynamic to *piano* followed by a *forte* - they can also indicate the difference between an orchestral ritornello and an accompanying passage, viz. No.8 bars 13, 16, 20, 36 etc. Editorial dynamics have been included in square brackets where they will be of assistance.

THE REHEARSAL PIANO ACCOMPANIMENT
This edition is provided with a new rehearsal accompaniment in which the material based on instrumental parts is in normal-size type and editorial realisation of the figured bass is in cue-size. It endeavours to embrace all of the orchestration, although it has not been possible to preserve every part at the correct pitch: but in this I am consistent with every other edition currently available. Figures have been given for all of the chords in the *secco* Recitative sections.

THE ORCHESTRAL SCORE AND PARTS
The Continuo parts (*Keyboard* and *Cello/Bass*) contain the full text of the Recitatives, whilst the other instrumental parts contain such word-cues as are helpful. The orchestral parts may be used for both 'period' instrument and 'modern' instrument performances.

NOTES
Flute At a late stage Bach introduced a flute, and changed some of the instrumentation accordingly. In the Adagio section of *Sinfonia* no.1 it replaced the solo oboe. In the soprano aria no. 4, which is in B minor, we find Bach preferring the obbligato to be played by a flute rather than by a violin, as he did in the Benedictus of the B Minor Mass. Either instrument is suitable.

Oboes Bach's requirements are for two oboes, with the first doubling *oboe d'amore* in the alto aria no. 8. Oboe 1 also has the music for the adagio section of *Sinfonia* no. 1, for those occasions when it will not be played by the flute.

Strings The optional violin solo in soprano aria no. 4 is included in the Violin 1 part, for those occasions when it will not be played by the flute.

Bassoon This part is similar to the Cello/Double Bass, apart from the fact that the bassoon has a solo obbligato at bb. 85-121 of *Sinfonia* no.1. It will be left to the conductor to decide in which arias the bassoon should play.

Keyboard Continuo This is the part from which the continuo should be played. The vocal score, though furnished with figures in the recitatives, is no adequate substitute, since the rest of its keyboard part is a piano reduction for rehearsal purposes. The *Keyboard Continuo* part contains the such figures as appear in the manuscript, and a new realisation which will be of enormous assistance to those not used to improvising from the figured bass.

Neil Jenkins
Hove, May 2003

1 Neil Jenkins, Preface to *J.S.Bach, Christmas Oratorio*, London, 1999
2 Werner Neumann, *Bach, Sämtliche Kantatentexte* Leipzig, 1974
3 Malcolm Boyd (editor), *Bach* Oxford Composer Companions, Oxford, 1999
4 Spitta, *Bach*, Vol.II, Leipzig, 1880
5 Wilhelm Rust, Preface to Vol. XXI of the Bach-Gesellschaft Edition, Leipzig, 1871
6 Diethard Hellman, Preface to *J.S. Bach, Oster-Oratorium*, Stuttgart, 1992

Easter Oratorio
Oster Oratorium

Piano reduction and translation by Neil Jenkins

JOHANN SEBASTIAN BACH
(BWV 249)

1 **SINFONIA**

© 2003 Novello & Company Limited

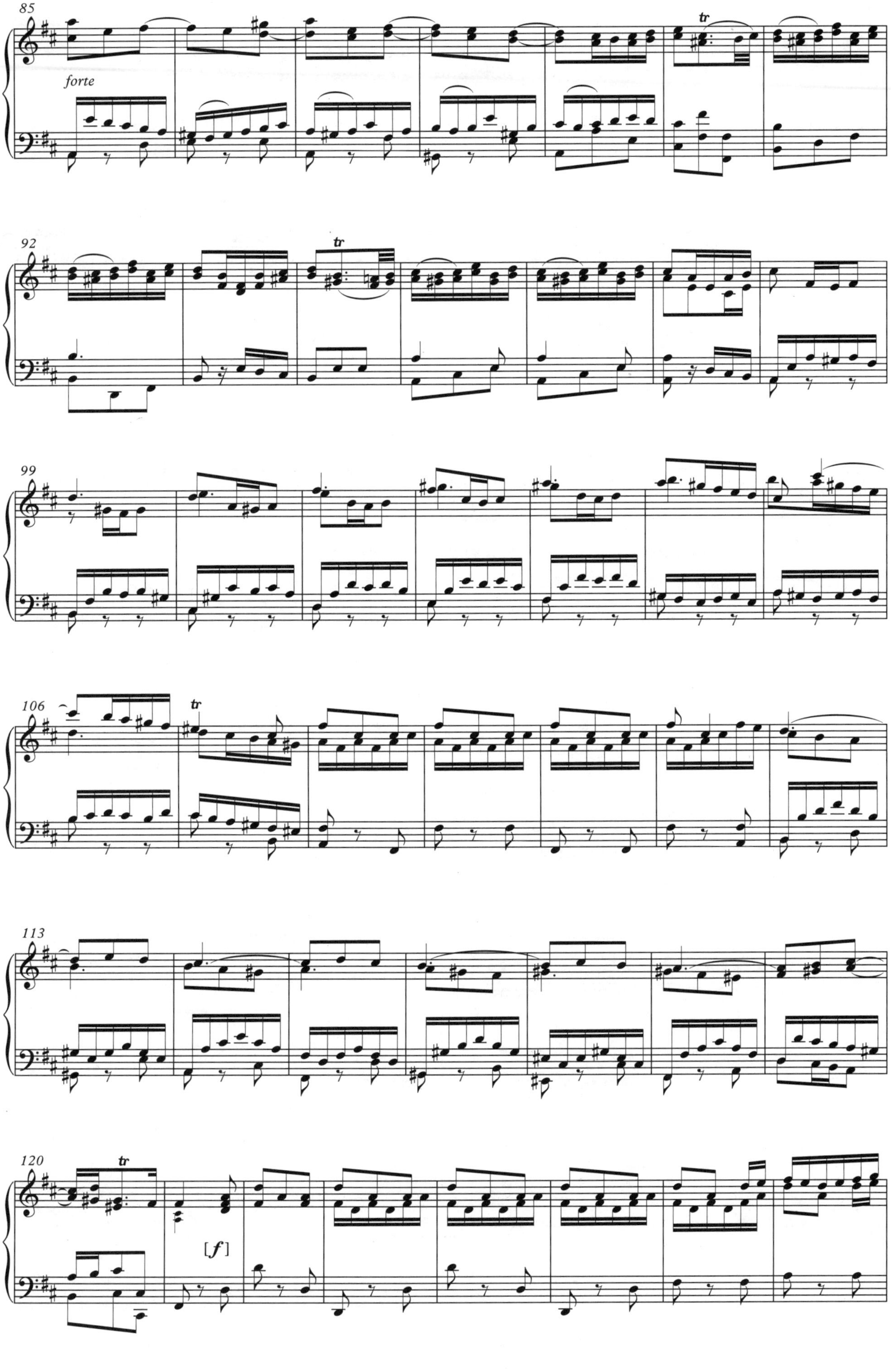
85
forte
tr
92
tr
99
106
tr
113
120
tr
[f]

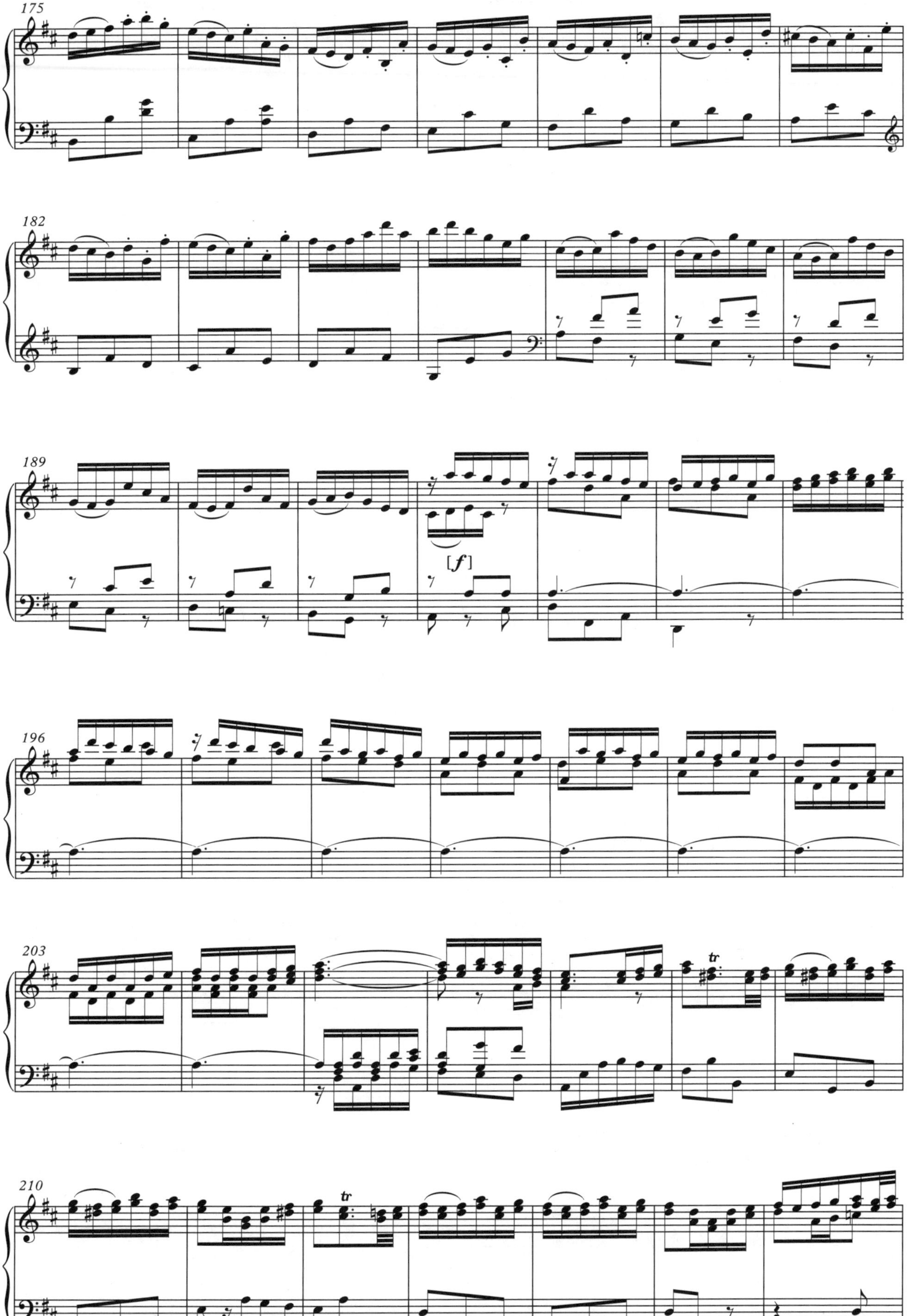
175
182
189
[f]
196
203
tr
210
tr

2 DUET & CHORUS

Version A - *Soloists only* - Tenor and Bass soloists sing to bar 160 and then *D.S.* to *Fine* at bar 120
Version B - *Soloists and Chorus* - Tenor and Bass soloists sing to bar 160 (chorus tacet). Performers ignore *Dal Segno* instruction. Chorus sing from bar 184 to end of movement.
Version C - *Soloists and Chorus* - Chorus sing to bar 96 (Tenor and Bass soloists tacet). Tenor and Bass soloists sing bars 120-160. Performers ignore *Dal Segno* instruction. Chorus sing from bar 184 to end of movement.

*Version A sing throughout; Version B sing to bar 160; Version C tacet to bar 96
†Version A tacet throughout; Version B tacet to bar 160; Version C sing throughout

*Fine for use with Version A only

Dal Segno al fine in Version A only; Versions B and C ignore *Dal Segno* instruction

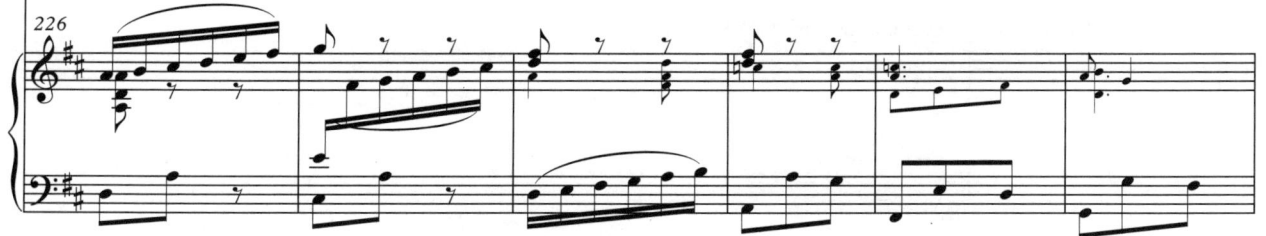

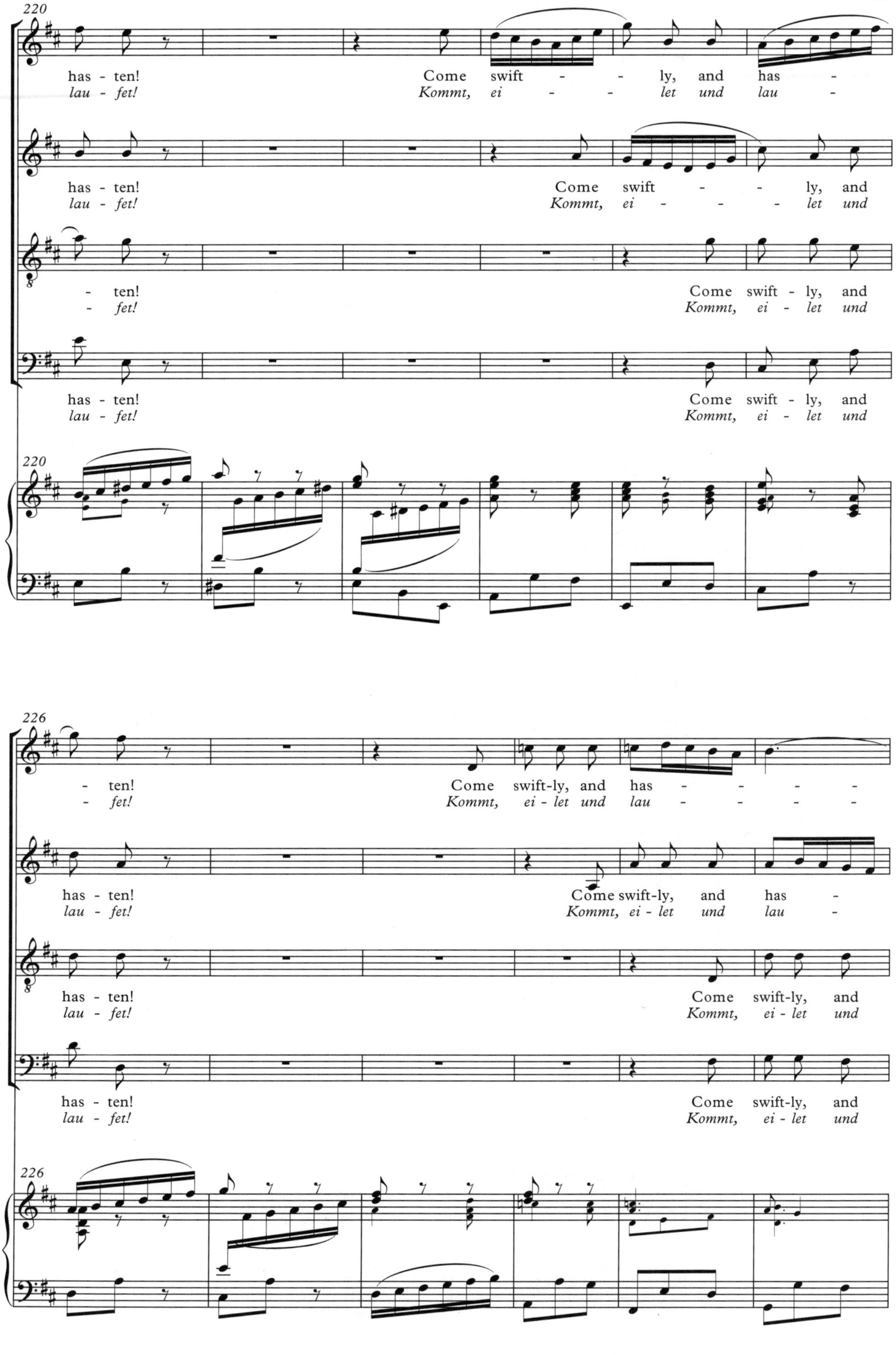
220
has - ten! Come swift - - ly, and has -
lau - fet! Kommt, ei - - let und lau -
has - ten! Come swift - - ly, and
lau - fet! Kommt, ei - - - let und
- ten! Come swift - ly, and
- fet! Kommt, ei - let und
has - ten! Come swift - ly, and
lau - fet! Kommt, ei - let und
220
226
- ten! Come swift-ly, and has - - - - -
- fet! Kommt, ei - let und lau - - - - -
has - ten! Come swift-ly, and has -
lau - fet! Kommt, ei - let und lau -
has - ten! Come swift-ly, and
lau - fet! Kommt, ei - let und
has - ten! Come swift-ly, and
lau - fet! Kommt, ei - let und
226

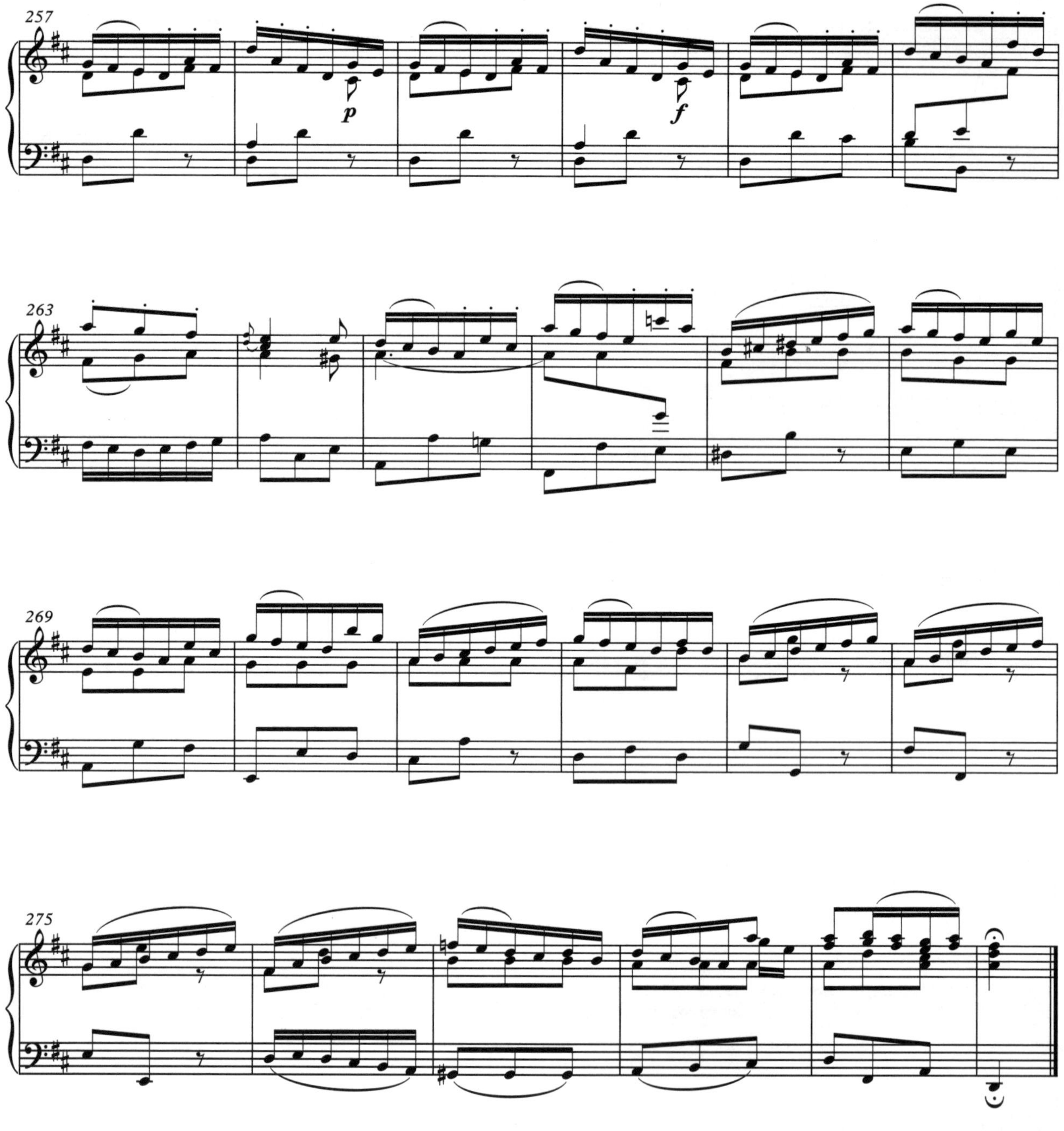
257
p
f
263
269
275

3 RECITATIVE

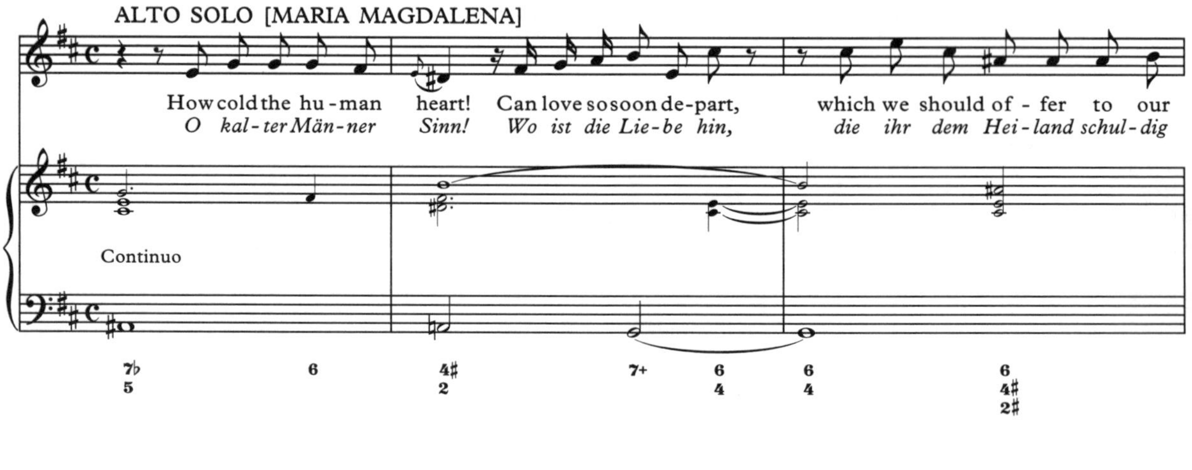
ALTO SOLO [MARIA MAGDALENA]
How cold the hu - man heart! Can love so soon de - part, which we should of - fer to our
O kal - ter Män - ner Sinn! Wo ist die Lie - be hin, die ihr dem Hei - land schul - dig
Continuo
7♭ 5
6
4♯ 2
7+
6 4
6 4
6 4♯ 2♯

28

4 SOPRANO SOLO

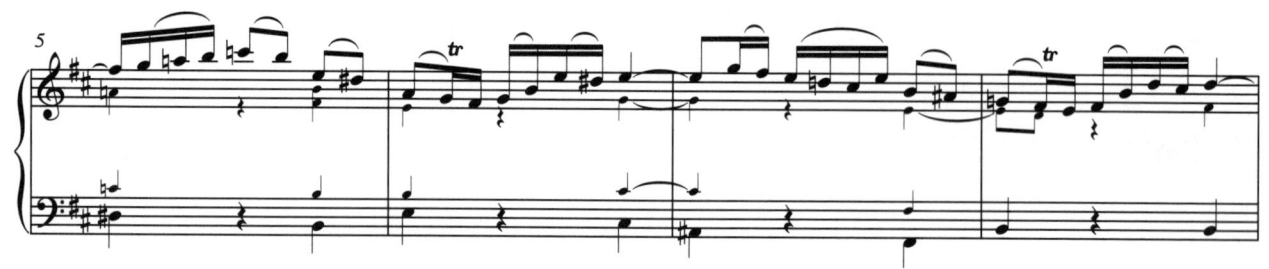

SOPRANO SOLO [MARIA JACOBI]

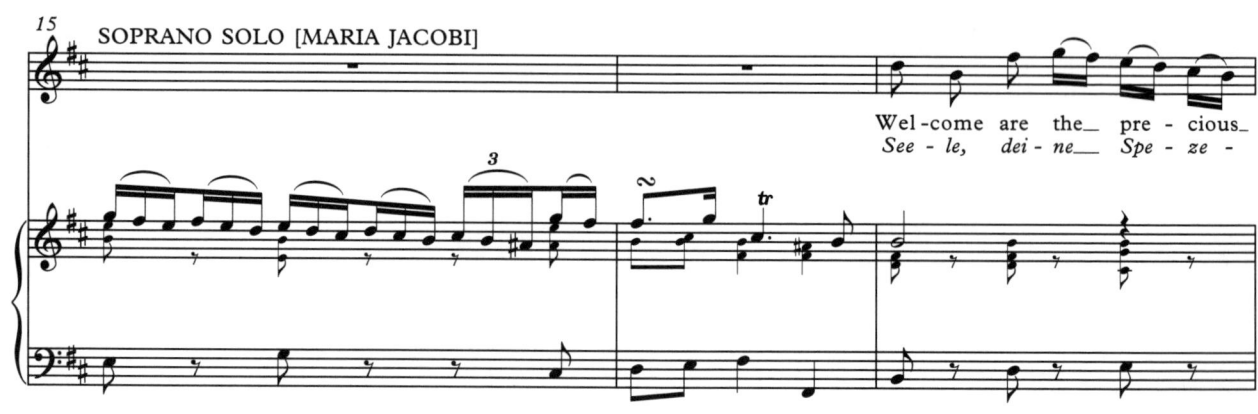

Wel-come are the pre-cious
See - le, dei - ne Spe - ze -

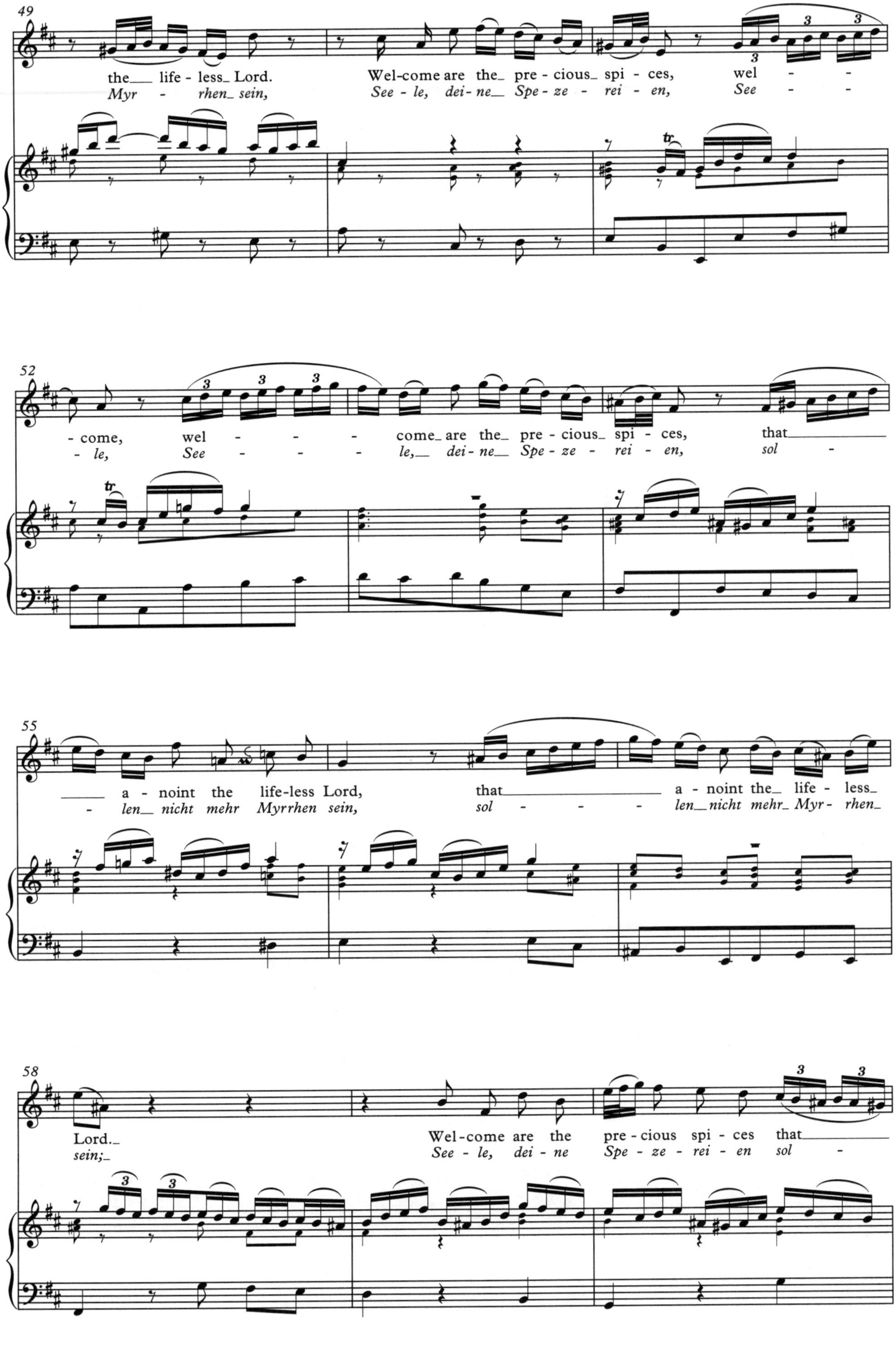
49
the__ life - less_ Lord. Wel-come are the_ pre - cious_ spi - ces, wel - -
Myr - rhen_ sein, See - le, dei- ne_ Spe- ze - rei - en, See - -
52
- come, wel - - - come_ are the_ pre - cious_ spi - ces, that
- le, See - - - le,_ dei - ne_ Spe - ze - rei - en, sol -
55
a - noint the life-less Lord, that a - noint the_ life - less_
- len_ nicht mehr Myrrhen sein, sol - - - len_ nicht mehr_ Myr - rhen_
58
Lord._ Wel-come are the pre - cious spi - ces that
sein;_ See - le, dei - ne Spe - ze - rei - en sol -

5 RECITATIVE

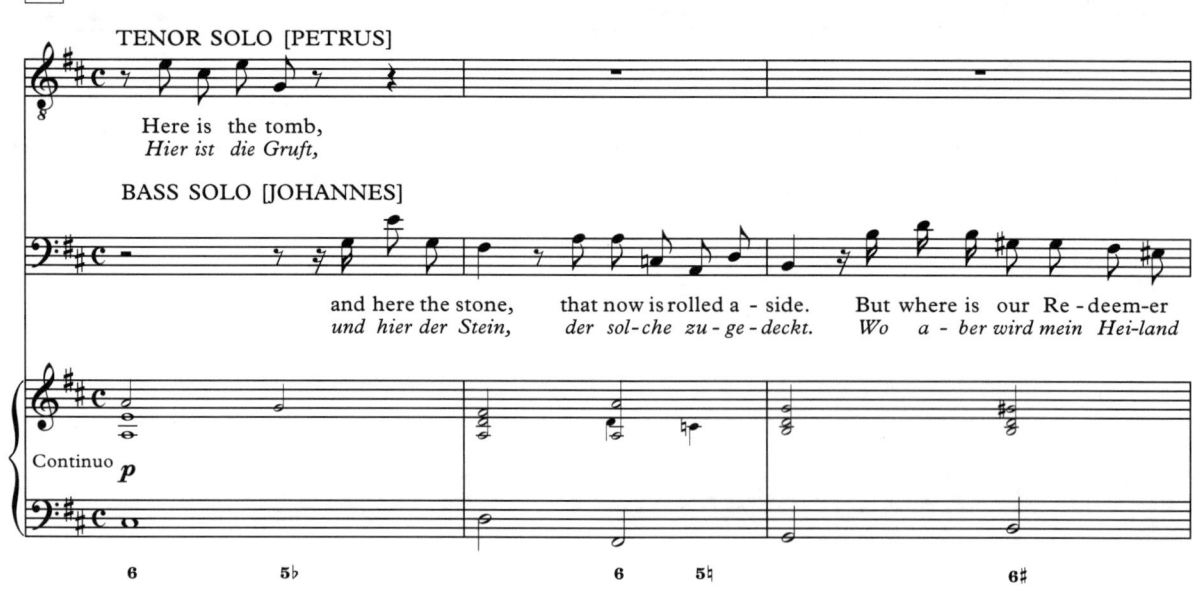

TENOR SOLO [PETRUS]
Here is the tomb,
Hier ist die Gruft,

BASS SOLO [JOHANNES]
and here the stone, that now is rolled aside. But where is our Redeemer
und hier der Stein, der solche zugedeckt. Wo aber wird mein Heiland

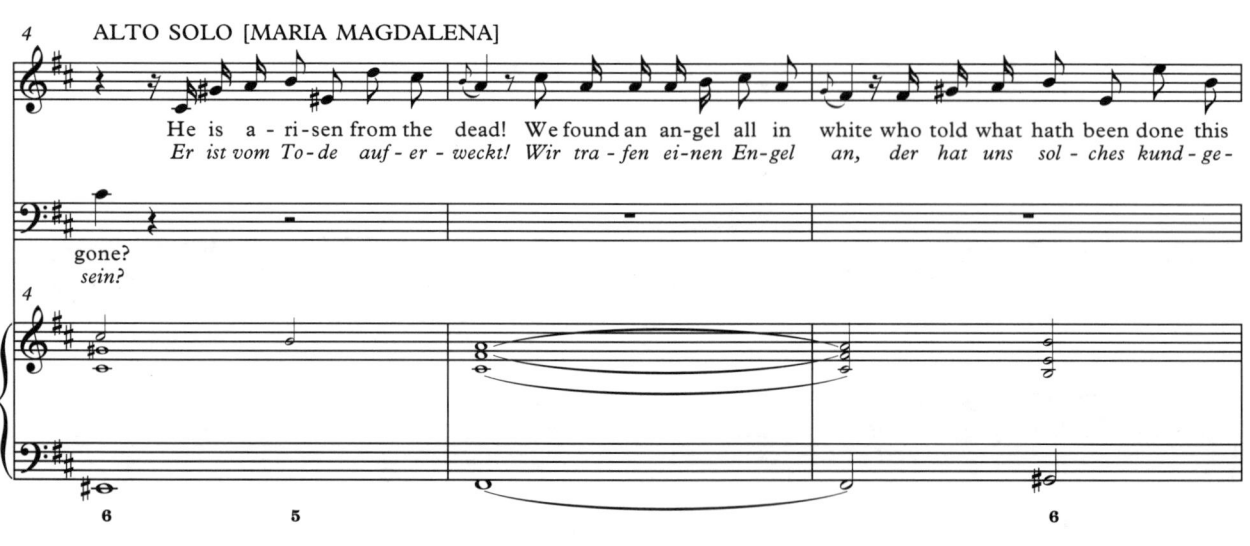

ALTO SOLO [MARIA MAGDALENA]
He is arisen from the dead! We found an angel all in white who told what hath been done this gone?
Er ist vom Tode auferweckt! Wir trafen einen Engel an, der hat uns solches kundgetan.

night.
TENOR SOLO
Behold, all doubt confounding, the linen that was wrapped around Him!
Hier seh ich mit Vergnügen das Schweißtuch abgewikkelt liegen.

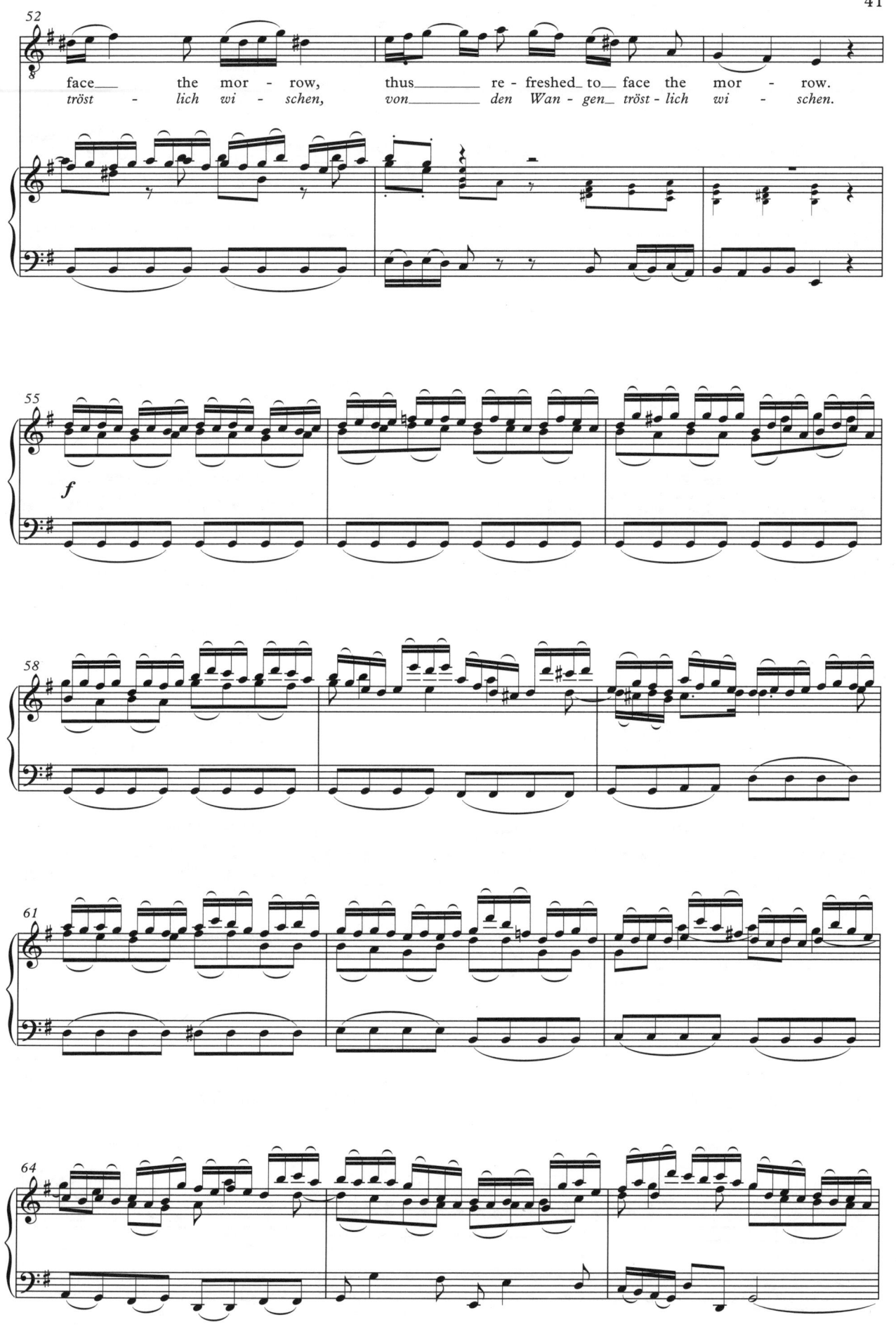

7 RECITATIVE
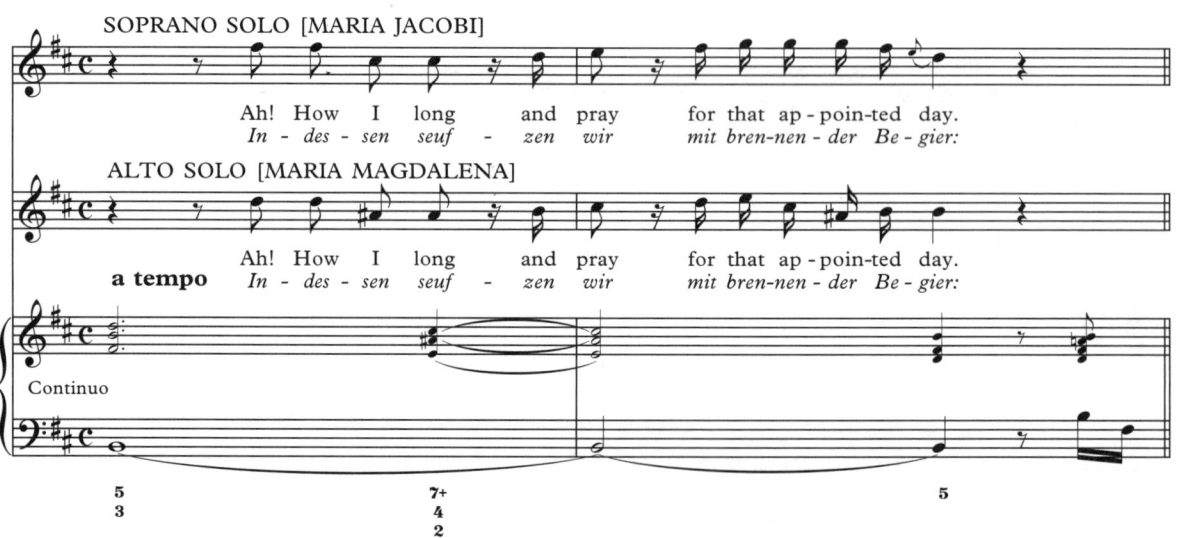

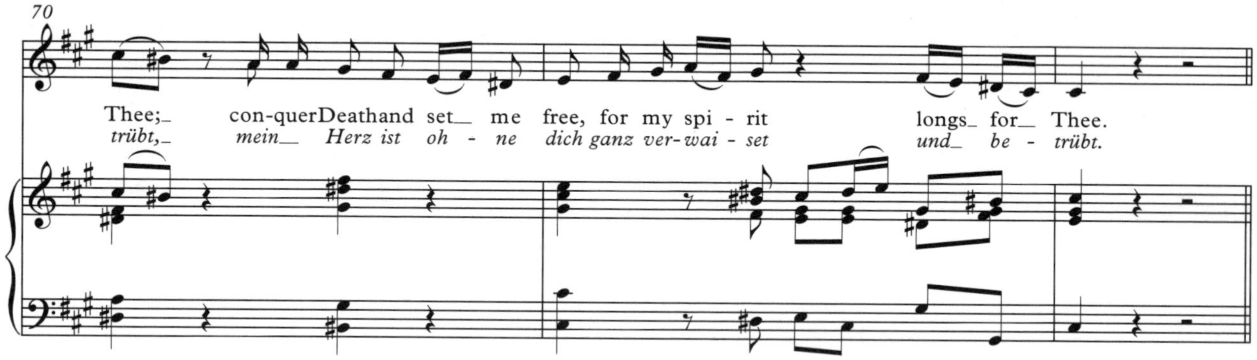
70
Thee;_ con-quer Death and set_ me free, for my spi - rit longs_ for_ Thee.
trübt,_ mein_ Herz ist oh - ne dich ganz ver-wai - set und_ be - trübt.

Da Capo al Fine

9 RECITATIVE

BASS SOLO [JOHANNES]

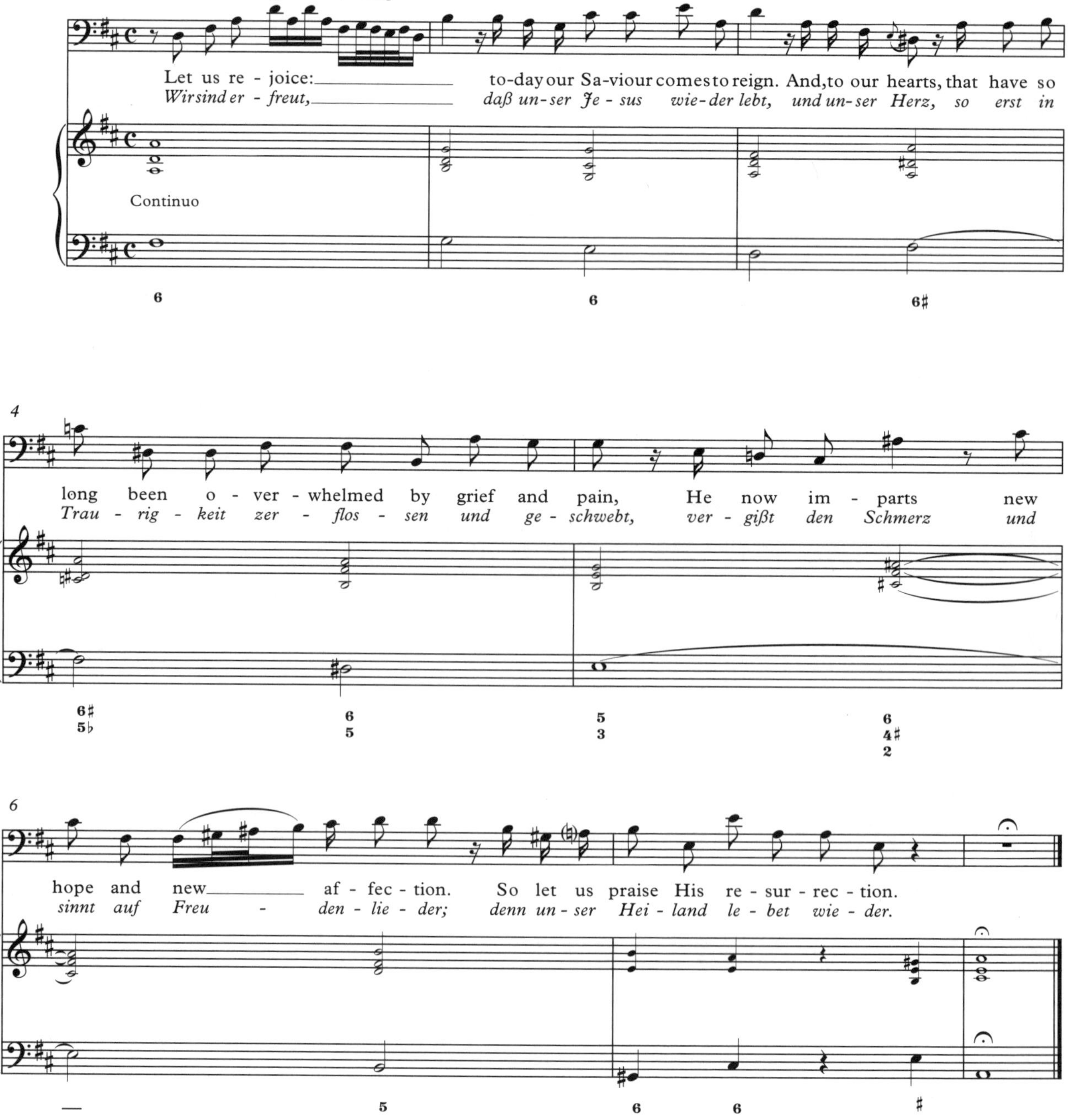
Let us re - joice:_ to-day our Sa-viour comes to reign. And, to our hearts, that have so
Wir sind er - freut,_ daß un-ser Je - sus wie-der lebt, und un-ser Herz, so erst in
Continuo
6 6 6♯
4
long been o - ver - whelmed by grief and pain, He now im - parts new
Trau - rig - keit zer - flos - sen und ge - schwebt, ver - gißt den Schmerz und
6♯ 5♭ 6 5 5 3 6 4♯ 2
6
hope and new_ af - fec - tion. So let us praise His re - sur - rec - tion.
sinnt auf Freu - den - lie - der; denn un - ser Hei - land le - bet wie - der.
— 5 6 6 ♯

-rious, the Lion of Judah has risen vic-
-gen, der Löwe von Juda kommt siegend ge-

ri - sen vic - to -
sie - gend ge - zo -

to - rious, the Lion of Judah has risen victorious!
zo - gen, der Löwe von Juda kommt siegend gezogen!

-on, the Lion of Judah has risen victorious!
-we, der Löwe von Juda kommt siegend gezogen!

-on, the Lion of Judah has risen victorious!
-we, der Löwe von Juda kommt siegend gezogen!

- - - rious, has ri - sen victorious!
- - - gen, kommt sie - gend gezogen!

APPENDIX

11 OPTIONAL CHORALE*

*Taken from Cantata 130 [transposed]. See Preface